# Bravo Phonics

## Cecilia Chan

Level 4

The Commercial Press

**Edited by:** Betty Wong

**Cover designed by:** Cathy Chiu

**Typeset by:** Rong Zhou

**Printing arranged by:** Kenneth Lung

## Bravo Phonics (Level 4)

| | |
|---|---|
| **Author:** | Cecilia Chan |
| **Publisher:** | The Commercial Press (H.K.) Ltd. |
| | 8/F, Eastern Central Plaza, 3 Yiu Hing Road, Shau Kei Wan, H.K. |
| | http://www.commercialpress.com.hk |
| **Distributor:** | THE SUP Publishing Logistics (H.K.) Ltd. |
| | 16/F, Tsuen Wan Industrial Building, 220-248 Texaco Road, |
| | Tsuen Wan, NT, Hong Kong |
| **Printer:** | Elegance Printing and Book Binding Co., Ltd. |
| | Block A, 4/F, Hoi Bun Industrial Building 6 Wing Yip Street, |
| | Kwun Tung Kowloon, Hong Kong |

© 2023 The Commercial Press (H.K.) Ltd.

First edition, First printing, July 2023

ISBN 978 962 07 0623 3

Printed in Hong Kong

Bravo Phonics Series is a special gift to all children – the ability to READ ENGLISH accurately and fluently! ENJOY!

# About the Author

The author, Ms Cecilia Chan, is a well-known English educator with many years of teaching experience. Passionate and experienced in teaching English, Ms Chan has taught students from over 30 schools in Hong Kong, including Marymount Primary School, Marymount Secondary School, Diocesan Boys' School, Diocesan Girls' School, St. Paul's Co-educational College, St. Paul's Co-educational College Primary School, St. Paul's College, St. Paul's Convent School (Primary and Secondary Sections), Belilios Public School, Raimondi College Primary Section, St. Clare's Primary School, St. Joseph's Primary School, St. Joseph's College, Pun U Association Wah Yan Primary School and other international schools. Many of Ms Chan's students have won prizes in Solo Verse Speaking, Prose Reading and Public Speaking at the Hong Kong Schools Speech Festival and

other interschool open speech contests. Driven by her passion in promoting English learning, Ms Chan has launched the Bravo Phonics Series (Levels 1-5) as an effective tool to foster a love of English reading and learning in children.

To all my
Beloved Students

# Acknowledgement

Many thanks to the Editor,
JY Ho, for her effort and
contribution to the editing of
the Bravo Phonics Series and
her assistance all along.

# Author's Words

The fundamental objective of phonics teaching is to develop step-by-step a child's ability to pronounce and recognize the words in the English language. Each phonic activity is a means to build up the child's power of word recognition until such power has been thoroughly exercised that word recognition becomes practically automatic.

Proper phonic training is highly important to young children especially those with English as a second language. It enables a child to acquire a large reading vocabulary in a comparatively short time and hence can happily enjoy fluent story reading. By giving phonics a place in the daily allotment of children's activities, they can be brought to a state of reading proficiency at an early age. Be patient, allow ample time for children to enjoy each and every phonic activity; if it is well and truly done, further steps will be taken easily and much more quickly.

Bravo Phonics Series has proven to be of value in helping young children reach the above objective and embark joyfully on the voyage of learning to read. It consists of five books of five levels,

covering all the letter sounds of the consonants, short and long vowels, diphthongs and blends in the English language. Bravo Phonics Series employs a step-by-step approach, integrating different learning skills through a variety of fun reading, writing, drawing, spelling and story-telling activities. There are quizzes, drills, tongue twisters, riddles and comprehension exercises to help consolidate all the letter sounds learnt. The QR code on each page enables a child to self-learn at home by following the instructions of Ms Chan while simultaneously practising the letter sounds through the example given.

The reward to teachers and parents will be a thousandfold when children gain self-confidence and begin to apply their phonic experiences to happy story reading.

# Contents

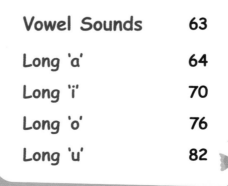

Quick Guide

 **Read**

 **Write**

 **Colour**

 **Draw**

 SCAN ME **Scan**

 Check

 Circle

 Join

 Say

 Spell

Hello, this is Ms Chan. How are you today?
Are you ready to learn Bravo Phonics?
Let's begin!

# Final Consonant Blends

| nd | mp | ch |
| nt | th | sh |
| st | sk | ts |
| ft | ck | tch |
| lt | nk | ght |
| lk | ng | |

# Final Consonant Blends

 Say the words on the right after me.

 Join each picture with the words that tell about it.

 •

• a bent pin

 •

• a sand hill

 •

• a small gift

 •

• a fat duck

 •       • a long belt

 •       • a green mask

 •       • a fish tank

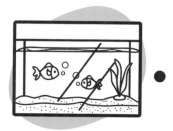 •       • a bright lamp

 Say the names of the pictures after me.

 Now colour the pictures.

3

# Final Consonant Blends

 Say the words on the right after me.

 Join each picture with the words that tell about it.

 •

• a big pouch

 •

• an egg in a nest

 •

• a gold ring

 •

• a hot bath

4

 •

• two foxes

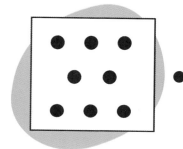 •

• a yellow dish

 •

• nine matches

 •

• eight dots

 Say the names of the pictures after me.

 Now colour the pictures.

5

# Final Consonant Blends

 Say the words in each row.

Choose a word from the box that rhymes with the words in each row.

 Write the word on the line.

---

grunt    rest    sift

hint    hand

---

gift    lift    rift    _____sift_____

land    band    sand    _____

best    test    nest    _____

runt    hunt    punt    _____

| sank | task | dish |
| ring | winch | |

mask  bask  flask  _____

sing  bing  sting  _____

tank  rank  blank  _____

inch  finch  pinch  _____

Now say the rhyming words in each row after me.

# Final Consonant Blends

 Say the words in each row.

Choose a word from the box that rhymes with the words in each row.

 Write the word on the line.

| mump    duck    stalk |
| kick    melt |

felt    belt    spelt    __melt__

talk    walk    chalk    _____

jump    lump    trump    _____

tick    sick    flick    _____

8

> match   flash   flints
> fight   tents

dash     mash     cash     _____

hints    tints    mints    _____

catch    batch    latch    _____

sight    might    tight    _____

 Now say the rhyming words in each row after me.

# Let's learn about Consonant Sounds!

# Initial Consonant Sounds

y

v

z

qu

# Initial Consonant Sounds

 Say the names of the pictures.

 Circle the correct sound with which each picture begins.

y  qu  v  z

z  v  y  qu

v  z  qu  y

qu  z  y  v

y  z  v  qu

 Say the names of the pictures after me.

  Now colour the pictures.

12

Say the names of the pictures.

 Circle the word that matches each picture.

tip
rip
zip

tilt
kilt
quilt

box
fox
tox

mellow
yellow
fellow

rest
test
vest

 Say the names of the pictures after me.

 Now colour the pictures.

13

Say the names of the pictures.

 Spell the name of each picture by writing the sound with which the picture begins.

_____olk          _____iolin          ____ ____ack

_____acht                    _____ox

 Spell and say the names of the picture after me.

  Now colour the pictures.

14

Say the names of the pictures.

 Spell the name of each picture by writing the sound with which the picture begins.

_____ ____ilt          _____awn          _____ero

_____ip          _____ase

 Spell and say the names of the picture after me.

 Now colour the pictures.

# Initial Consonant Clusters

| | |
|---|---|
| wh | st |
| sh | sp |
| ch | sk |
| th | sn |

# Initial Consonant Clusters

 Say the words in each row.

 Circle those words that begin with the same sound.

when what which     how

ship     shop     chop     shoe

chap     with     chip     chan

thick     thin     stop     think

18

| | | | |
|---|---|---|---|
| stop | step | stamp | top |
| span | pin | spit | spin |
| skip | skin | clam | skid |
| snap | clap | snug | snip |

Now say the words in each row that begin with the same sound after me.

19

# Initial Consonant Clusters

 Say the words in each row.

 Circle those words that begin with the same sound.

( skirt )   ( skew )   shout   ( skate )

which   whack   whine   thick

steep   thank   stump   stitch

this   that   those   tank

shut    sheep    show    chuck

spine    spill    plant    spider

snake    rake    snatch    snap

chick    chose    check    where

 Now say the words in each row that begin with the same sound after me.

# Are you ready for more practice?
## Let's begin!

# Fun Drawing

# Fun Drawing

 Read the words in each box after me.

 Guess what 'the thing' is and draw it.

 Colour your pictures.

A thing to drink from

A thing to skip with

25

# Fun Drawing

 Read the words in each box after me.

 Guess what 'the thing' is and draw it.

 Colour your pictures.

## A thing to sit on

26

A thing to cut with

# Fun Drawing

 Read the words in each box after me.

 Guess what 'the thing' is and draw it.

 Colour your pictures.

A thing to bathe in

A thing to sleep on

Read the words in each box after me.

 Guess what 'the thing' is and draw it.

 Colour your pictures.

A thing to put flowers in

A thing to put a stamp on

Are you ready for the challenge?
Let's begin!

# Let's Think

# Let's Think

 Read the questions below and look for the answers from the pictures.

 Write each answer in a sentence.

The first one is done for you.

## Which ship is bigger?

**This ship is bigger.**

That ship

This ship

# Which chick is thinner?

_____

_____

## That chick

## This chick

 Let's check the answers.

# Let's Think

 Read the questions below and look for the answers from the pictures.

 Write each answer in a sentence.

## Which snake is longer?

_____

_____

**That snake**

**This snake**

Which shirt is yellow in colour?

_____

_____

That shirt

This shirt

 Let's check the answers.

# Let's Think

 Read the questions below and look for the answers from the pictures.

 Write each answer in a sentence.

## Which spider has a web?

_____

_____

**This spider**

**That spider**

38

Which chair is taller?

_____

_____

## This chair

## That chair

 Let's check the answers.

# Are you ready for more practice?
# Let's begin!

# Initial Consonant Clusters

| sl | br |
|----|----|
| cl | dr |
| fl | gr |
| bl | pr |
| pl | tr |

Say the words in each row.

 Circle those words that begin with the same sound.

| | | | |
|---|---|---|---|
| slip | slab | that | slap |
| clap | climb | clip | step |
| flag | flop | black | flip |
| blue | sleep | blot | blink |
| play | plan | tape | plum |

**42**

| | | | |
|---|---|---|---|
| brag | brick | brush | drag |
| drum | drink | crane | drain |
| grin | green | preen | grow |
| pray | press | prick | tray |
| tram | these | trick | true |

Now say the words in each row that begin with the same sound after me.

# Initial Consonant Clusters

 Say the words in each row.

 Circle those words that begin with the same sound.

| | | | |
|---|---|---|---|
| class | flow | cliff | click |
| drill | droll | grunt | dress |
| bluff | bliss | bless | please |
| press | track | print | prank |
| sluff | slope | blank | slang |

44

grill     grass     prune     group

fluff     fleet     flick     glow

troll     cloud     truff     treat

plant     plane     green     pleat

brass     trump     bring     brave

 Now say the words in each row that
begin with the same sound after me.

Are you ready for more challenges?
Let's begin!

# Fun Drawing

Read the words in each box after me.

 Guess what 'the place' is and draw it.

 Colour your pictures.

A place to live in

A place to swim in

A place to buy food

49

# Fun Drawing

 Read the words in each box after me.

 Guess what 'the place' is and draw it.

 Colour your pictures.

A place to read books

50

A place to play football

A place to buy clothes

# Fun Drawing

 Read the words in each box after me.

 Guess what 'the place' is and draw it.

 Colour your pictures.

A place to play the swing

A place to sing songs

A place to eat breakfast

# Are you ready for more practice?
## Let's begin!

# Let's Think

# Let's Think

Read the questions below and look for the answers from the pictures.

Write each answer in a sentence.

## Which flower has five petals?

_____

_____

**Your flower**

**My flower**

56

# Which clock is blue in colour?

_____

_____

# Your clock

# His clock

 Let's check the answers.

Read the questions below and look for the answers from the pictures.

 Write each answer in a sentence.

## Which dress is clean?

_____

_____

**Her dress**

**Your dress**

Which tram is green in colour?

_____

_____

His tram

Our tram

 Let's check the answers.

# Let's Think

 Read the questions below and look for the answers from the pictures.

 Write each answer in a sentence.

## Which plant is taller?

_____

_____

**Their plant**

**Our plant**

Which sheep has more wool?

_____

_____

**Our sheep**

**Their sheep**

 Let's check the answers.

# Let's learn about Vowel Sounds!

# Vowel Sounds

Long 'a'

Long 'i'

Long 'o'

Long 'u'

# Long vowel 'a'

 Say the words in each row.

 Circle those words that rhyme with the first one.

cake    (lake)    (make)    late

game    same    some    came

date    tape    late    plate

tape    grape    drape    made

spade    made    rake    fade

snake    scale    take    fake

plane    mane    lane    same

blaze    craze    doze    daze

 Now say the words in each row that rhyme after me.

# Long vowel 'a'

 Say the words in the box.

 Find the words that match each picture and write them on the line.

a plane   a gate   a cake
a lake   a maze

_____

_____

_____

_____

_____

 Say the names of the pictures after me.

 Now colour the pictures.

# Long vowel 'a'

 Say the words in the box.

 Find the word that matches each picture and write it on the line.

rakes    grapes    tapes
plates    snakes

_____

_____

_____

_____

_____

 Say the names of the pictures after me.

 Now colour the pictures.

# Long vowel 'i'

 Say the words in each row.

 Circle those words that rhyme with the first one.

| like | bake | (bike) | (spike) |

| hide | ride | rude | slide |

| wine | fine | dine | sign |

| time | dime | date | mime |

**70**

stile      mine      file      mile

price      rice      dice      race

white      bite      kite      wife

stripe      strap      ripe      pipe

 Now say the words in each row that rhyme after me.

Say the words in the box.

 Find the words that match each picture and write them on the line.

a bike  a dice  a ride
a stile  a bite

_____

_____

_____

_____

_____

 Say the names of the pictures after me.

 Now colour the pictures.

# Long vowel 'i'

Say the words in the box.

Find the word that matches each picture and write it on the line.

> **files   pipes   tiles**
> **slides   kites**

_____

_____

_____

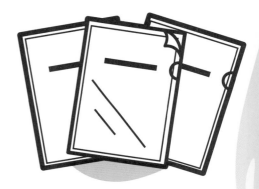

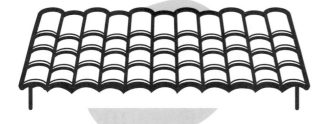

_____

_____

 Say the names of the pictures after me.

 Now colour the pictures.

# Long vowel 'o'

 Say the words in each row.

 Circle those words that rhyme with the first one.

coke    (poke)    pope    (broke)

bone    lose    cone    tone

rode    mode    code    made

hole    mile    mole    dole

stone   phone   throne   time

home   done   dome   tome

rope   hope   cope   cape

rose   dose   rise   hose

 Now say the words in each row that rhyme after me.

# Long vowel 'o'

 Say the words in the box.

 Find the words that match each picture and write them on the line.

a throne    a coke    a hole
a dome    a hose

_____

_____

_____

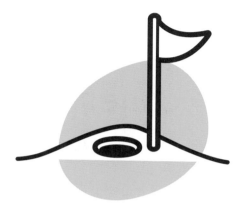

_____

_____

 Say the names of the pictures after me.

 Now colour the pictures.

# Long vowel 'o'

 Say the words in the box.

 Find the word that matches each picture and write it on the line.

> cones   bones   stones
> roses   ropes

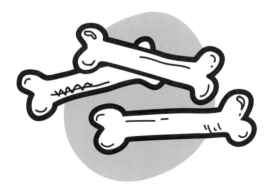

_____

_____

_____

_____

_____

 Say the names of the pictures after me.

 Now colour the pictures.

# Long vowel 'u'

 Say the words in each row.

 Circle those words that rhyme with the first one.

clue    (true)    but    (blue)

tune    dune    prune    tone

duke    puke    nuke    nude

blue    tree    glue    flu

use    fuse    fuss    muse

 Now say the words in each row that rhyme after me.

Say the words in the box.

 Find the word that matches each picture and write it on the line.

| |
|---|
| **prunes    tunes    dukes** <br> **dunes    glues** |

_____

_____

_____

_____

_____

 Say the names of the pictures after me.

 Now colour the pictures.

# Are you ready for the challenge?
## Let's begin!

# Fun Drawing

Read the words in each box after me.

 Draw as you are told to do.

 Colour your pictures.

## There are two dogs.
## Give each dog a bone.

There are five roses.
Colour them in five colours.

# Fun Drawing

 Read the words in each box after me.

 Draw as you are told to do.

 Colour your pictures.

Jane wants to fly a kite.
Give her a kite.

90

Sue has baked a cake.
Write her name on it.

# Fun Drawing

 Read the words in each box after me.

 Draw as you are told to do.

 Colour your pictures.

# Watch out! There is a snake in the hole.
# Draw a snake in it.

Dave loves to drink coke.
Give him a coke.

# Fun Drawing

 Read the words in each box after me.

 Draw as you are told to do.

 Colour your pictures.

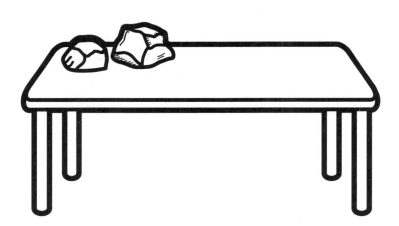

## There are two stones on the table.
## Draw four more stones on it.

94

There is a throne.
Draw a king sitting on it.

# Fun Drawing

 Read the words in each box after me.

 Draw as you are told to do.

 Colour your pictures.

It is a fine day.

Draw a plane in the sky.

June likes to play on the slide.
Draw June on the slide.

# Fun Drawing

 Read the words in each box after me.

 Draw as you are told to do.

 Colour your pictures.

The fireman wants to put out the blaze.
Give the fireman a hose.

It is now nine o'clock.
Draw the time on the clock.

Are you ready for more practice?
Let's begin!

# Diphthongs

ea

ee

ai

ay

oa

oe

# ea

 Read the words in each box after me.

 Circle the word that matches each picture and write it on the line.

peach
teach
reach

beans
means
cleans

_____

_____

cream
dream
beam

beat
seat
meat

_____

_____

  Say the names of the pictures after me.

 Now colour the pictures.

# ee

 Read the words in each box after me.

 Circle the word that matches each picture and write it on the line.

bee
see
tree

sleep
sheep
steep

feel
heel
reel

breed
feed
seed

 Say the names of the pictures after me.

 Now colour the pictures.

103

## ea  ee

 Fill in the missing sounds of the words to make them all rhyme with each other.

The first one is done for you.

| | | |
|---|---|---|
| s<u>ea</u> | p<u>e</u> a | t<u>e</u> a |
| | fl<u>e</u> a | |
| m<u>ea</u>t | h__t | b__t |
| | s__t | |
| s<u>ee</u> | b__ | tr__ |
| | thr__ | |
| f<u>ee</u>t | b__t | m__t |
| | fl__t | |

104

b<u>ea</u>n    m\_\_\_n    l\_\_\_n

          cl\_\_\_n

h<u>ee</u>l    f\_\_\_l    r\_\_\_l

          st\_\_\_l

b<u>ea</u>m    dr\_\_\_m    cr\_\_\_m

          st\_\_\_m

p<u>ee</u>p    sh\_\_\_p    sl\_\_\_p

          st\_\_\_p

 Now say the rhyming words in each row after me.

# ai

 Read the words in each box after me.

 Circle the word that matches each picture and write it on the line.

| rain |
| train |
| vain |

_____

| pail |
| tail |
| snail |

_____

| paint |
| faint |
| saint |

_____

| chain |
| drain |
| strain |

_____

 Say the names of the pictures after me.

 Now colour the pictures.

# ay

 Read the words in each box after me.

 Circle the word that matches each picture and write it on the line.

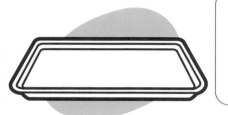

say
tray
day

bay
way
clay

may
stay
play

spray
pray
stray

 Say the names of the pictures after me.

 Now colour the pictures.

107

# ai   ay

Fill in the missing sounds of the words to make them all rhyme with each other.

r<u>ai</u>n          p___n          v___n
                   tr___n

t<u>ai</u>l          p___l          f___l
                   sn___l

d<u>ay</u>          s___           m___
                   w___

pl<u>ay</u>          cl___          st___
                   str___

m**ai**d    p___d    r___d
            l__d

b**ay**     g___    h__
            l__

r**ai**l    m___l    s___l
            w__l

dr**ai**n   st___n   pl___n
            spr___n

 Now say the rhyming words in each row after me.

# oa

 Read the words in each box after me.

 Circle the word that matches each picture and write it on the line.

coat
moat
boat

load
toad
road

_____

_____

toast
roast
boast

goal
foal
coal

_____

_____

 Say the names of the pictures after me.

 Now colour the pictures.

# oa oe

 Read the words in each box after me.

 Circle the word that matches each picture and write it on the line.

woes
foes
toes

foam
roam
loam

doe
toe
foe

toe
hoe
woe

 Say the names of the pictures after me.

 Now colour the pictures.

# oa oe

 Fill in the missing sounds of the words to make them all rhyme with each other.

**c<u>oa</u>t**     b___t     m___t

             g___t

**r<u>oa</u>d**     t___d     l___d

             g___d

**t<u>oe</u>**     f___     w___

             d___

**w<u>oe</u>s**     d___s     t___s

             f___s

112

loam    f___m    r___m

foal    g___l    c___l

moan    l___n    gr___n

roast    b___st    c___st

 Now say the rhyming words in each row after me.

113

# Rhyming Words are fun!
## Let's begin!

# Rhyming Words

## The 'y' and 'ie' Sounds

 y ie

 Say the words in each row.

 Circle those words that rhyme with the first one.

| my | by | trip | fry | buy |
|----|----|------|-----|-----|

| tie | hid | die | pie | lie |
|-----|-----|-----|-----|-----|

| cry | dry | say | why | fly |
|-----|-----|-----|-----|-----|

| lies | tries | leads | dries | fries |
|------|-------|-------|-------|-------|

| buy | why | bay | cry | try |
|-----|-----|-----|-----|-----|

  Now say the words in each row that rhyme after me.

 **y    ie**

 Say the words in each box after me.

 Find the words that match each picture and write them on the line.

| a pie | a fly |
|-------|-------|

| a cry | a tie |
|-------|-------|

_____

_____                    _____

 Say the names of the pictures after me.

 Now colour the pictures.

117

 Say the sentence in each box.

 Find the sentence that matches each picture and write it on the line.

> # He tries on the tie.

> # She buys a pie.

_____

_____

_____

_____

 Say the sentences after me.

 Now colour the pictures.

# Rhyming Words are fun!
# Let's begin!

# Rhyming Words

The 'all' and 'aw'
Sounds

# all aw

 Say the words in each row.

 Circle those words that rhyme with the first one.

| all | tail | ball | fall | call |

| jaw | saw | sea | paw | raw |

| dawn | law | pawn | lawn | prawn |

| wall | bell | hall | tall | mall |

| hall | wall | stall | smell | small |

  Now say the words in each row that rhyme after me.

Say the words in each box after me.

 Find the words that match each picture and write them on the line.

the jaw    the hall    the lawn

the stall    the prawn

 Say the names of the pictures after me.

 Now colour the pictures.

123

Say the words in each box after me.

 Find the words that match each picture and write them on the line.

A tall wall falls

A small prawn on the lawn

_____

_____

 Say the words after me.

 Now colour the pictures.

125

Are you ready for the Quizzes?
Let's start!

# Quizzes

The words in each row rhyme with each other.

Write another word that rhymes with them on the line.

bee    see    _____

foe    woe    _____

say    may    _____

pea    tea    _____

rail    pail    _____

load    road    _____

boat    moat    _____

peep    sheep    _____

 Check your answers with
the answer key.

Score

/8

129

The words in each row rhyme with each other.

 Write another word that rhymes with them on the line.

stay    clay    _____

mean    clean    _____

meet    beet    _____

train    vain    _____

reach   peach   _____

seed   reed   _____

woes   toes   _____

roam   loam   _____

 Check your answers with
the answer key.

Score

/8

The words in each row rhyme with each other.

 Write another word that rhymes with them on the line.

try     fry     _____

lie     pie     _____

tall     fall     _____

lawn     pawn     _____

lap map _____

tell bell _____

sip tip _____

rot not _____

cut gut _____

 Check your answers with the answer key.

 Score /8

 133

Read each question.

 Circle the correct answer.

Can you see this page?          Yes    No

Can you see the rain?          Yes    No

Can you hear the bell?          Yes    No

Can you hear the sun?          Yes    No

Can you hear the stars?                 Yes   No

Can you see the clouds?                 Yes   No

Can you hear sounds?                    Yes   No

Can you see with your nose?             Yes   No

 Let's check the answers.

Score

/8

135

Read each question.

 Circle the correct answer.

Can you read a book?　　　Yes　No

Can you read a chair?　　　Yes　No

Can you hear a dog bark?　　Yes　No

Can you hear a song?　　　　Yes　No

Can you smell a flower?  Yes  No

Can you smell light?  Yes  No

Can you touch the tree?  Yes  No

Can you touch your hair?  Yes  No

 Let's check the answers.

Score

/8

# Quiz 14.6

 Read each question.

 Circle the correct answer.

Can you taste sugar?                Yes    No

Can you taste air?                  Yes    No

Can you feel the wind?              Yes    No

Can you feel the tie?               Yes    No

Can we hear with our ears?        Yes   No

Can we smell with our mouth?      Yes   No

Can we feel with our fingers?     Yes   No

Can we taste with our tongue?     Yes   No

 Let's check the answers.

# Fun Drawing

Choose your favourite pictures from the book and draw them in the shapes.

Enjoy!

141

Well done, students! You can check your answers with the Answer Key.

# Answer Key

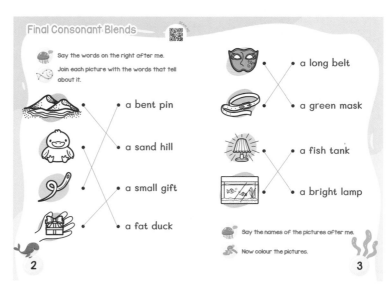

## Final Consonant Blends

🪼 Say the words on the right after me.

🐟 Join each picture with the words that tell about it.

- a bent pin
- a sand hill
- a small gift
- a fat duck

- a long belt
- a green mask
- a fish tank
- a bright lamp

🪼 Say the names of the pictures after me.

🐟 Now colour the pictures.

2

3

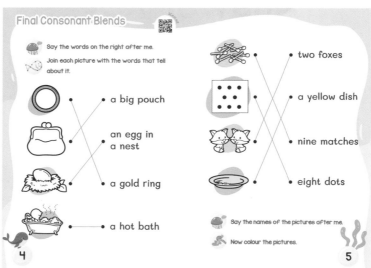

## Final Consonant Blends

🪼 Say the words on the right after me.

🐟 Join each picture with the words that tell about it.

- a big pouch
- an egg in a nest
- a gold ring
- a hot bath

- two foxes
- a yellow dish
- nine matches
- eight dots

🪼 Say the names of the pictures after me.

🐟 Now colour the pictures.

4

5

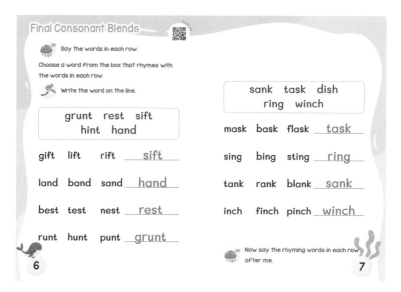

## Final Consonant Blends

🪼 Say the words in each row.

Choose a word from the box that rhymes with the words in each row.

🐟 Write the word on the line.

> grunt   rest   sift
> hint   hand

gift   lift   rift   __sift__

land   band   sand   __hand__

best   test   nest   __rest__

runt   hunt   punt   __grunt__

> sank   task   dish
> ring   winch

mask   bask   flask   __task__

sing   bing   sting   __ring__

tank   rank   blank   __sank__

inch   finch   pinch   __winch__

🪼 Now say the rhyming words in each row after me.

6

7

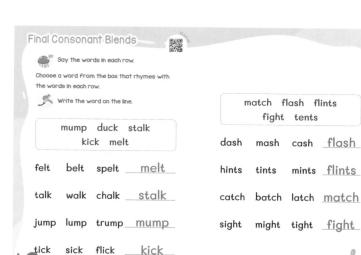

## Final Consonant Blends

🪼 Say the words in each row.

Choose a word from the box that rhymes with the words in each row.

🐙 Write the word on the line.

| mump | duck | stalk |
| kick | melt | |

felt    belt    spelt    __melt__

talk    walk    chalk    __stalk__

jump    lump    trump    __mump__

tick    sick    flick    __kick__

8

| match | flash | flints |
| fight | tents | |

dash    mash    cash    __flash__

hints    tints    mints    __flints__

catch    batch    latch    __match__

sight    might    tight    __fight__

🪼 Now say the rhyming words in each row after me.

9

## Initial Consonant Sounds

🪼 Say the names of the pictures.

⭕ Circle the correct sound with which each picture begins.

y  qu  v  z          z  v  y  qu          v  z  qu  y

qu  z  y  v          y  z  v  qu

🪼 Say the names of the pictures after me.

🐙 Now colour the pictures.

12

🪼 Say the names of the pictures.

⭕ Circle the word that matches each picture.

tip          tilt          box
rip          kilt          fox
zip          quilt         tox

mellow       rest
yellow       test
fellow       vest

🪼 Say the names of the pictures after me.

🐙 Now colour the pictures.

13

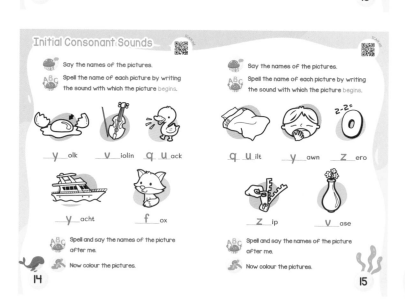

## Initial Consonant Sounds

🪼 Say the names of the pictures.

🔤 Spell the name of each picture by writing the sound with which the picture begins.

__y__ olk          __v__ iolin          __q u__ ack

__y__ acht          __f__ ox

🔤 Spell and say the names of the picture after me.

🐙 Now colour the pictures.

14

🪼 Say the names of the pictures.

🔤 Spell the name of each picture by writing the sound with which the picture begins.

__q u__ ilt          __y__ awn          __z__ ero

__z__ ip          __v__ ase

🔤 Spell and say the names of the picture after me.

🐙 Now colour the pictures.

15

145

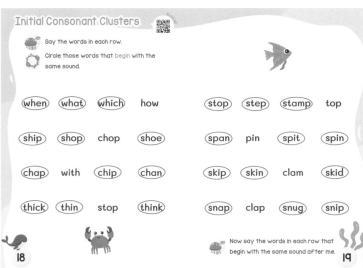

## Initial Consonant Clusters

Say the words in each row.

Circle those words that begin with the same sound.

(when) (what) (which) how     (stop) (step) (stamp) top

(ship) (shop) chop (shoe)     (span) pin (spit) (spin)

(chap) with (chip) (chan)     (skip) (skin) clam (skid)

(thick) (thin) stop (think)     (snap) clap (snug) (snip)

18

Now say the words in each row that begin with the same sound after me.

19

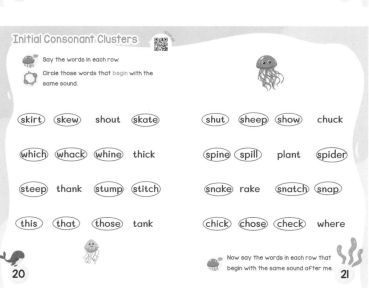

## Initial Consonant Clusters

Say the words in each row.

Circle those words that begin with the same sound.

(skirt) (skew) shout (skate)     (shut) (sheep) (show) chuck

(which) (whack) (whine) thick     (spine) (spill) plant (spider)

(steep) thank (stump) (stitch)     (snake) rake (snatch) (snap)

(this) (that) (those) tank     (chick) (chose) (check) where

20

Now say the words in each row that begin with the same sound after me.

21

## Fun Drawing

Read the words in each box after me.

Guess what 'the thing' is and draw it.

Colour your pictures.

A thing to drink from

Suggested Answer

A thing to skip with

Suggested Answer

24

25

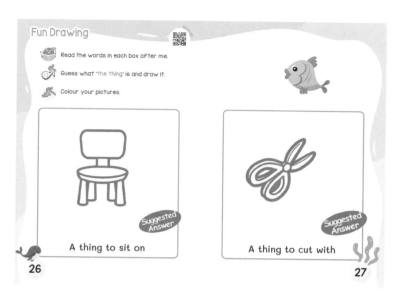

## Fun Drawing

- Read the words in each box after me.
- Guess what 'the thing' is and draw it.
- Colour your pictures.

*Suggested Answer*

A thing to sit on

26

*Suggested Answer*

A thing to cut with

27

## Fun Drawing

- Read the words in each box after me.
- Guess what 'the thing' is and draw it.
- Colour your pictures.

*Suggested Answer*

A thing to bathe in

28

*Suggested Answer*

A thing to sleep on

29

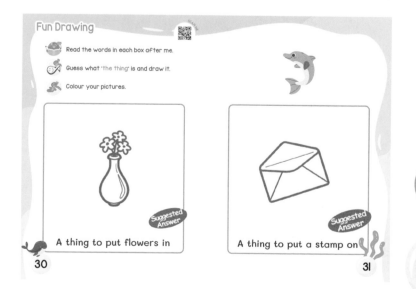

## Fun Drawing

- Read the words in each box after me.
- Guess what 'the thing' is and draw it.
- Colour your pictures.

*Suggested Answer*

A thing to put flowers in

30

*Suggested Answer*

A thing to put a stamp on

31

147

Read the questions below and look for the answers from the pictures.

Write each answer in a sentence.

The first one is done for you.

Which ship is bigger?

**This ship is bigger.**

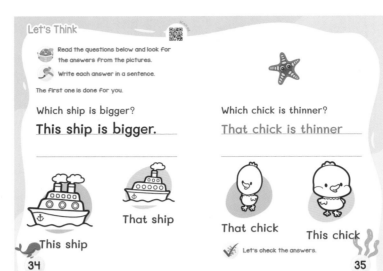

That ship

This ship

34

Which chick is thinner?

That chick is thinner

That chick

This chick

Let's check the answers.

35

Read the questions below and look for the answers from the pictures.

Write each answer in a sentence.

Which snake is longer?

This snake is longer.

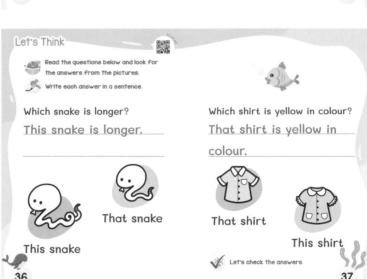

That snake

This snake

36

Which shirt is yellow in colour?

That shirt is yellow in colour.

That shirt

This shirt

Let's check the answers.

37

Read the questions below and look for the answers from the pictures.

Write each answer in a sentence.

Which spider has a web?

This spider has a web.

That spider

This spider

38

Which chair is taller?

That chair is taller.

This chair

That chair

Let's check the answers.

39

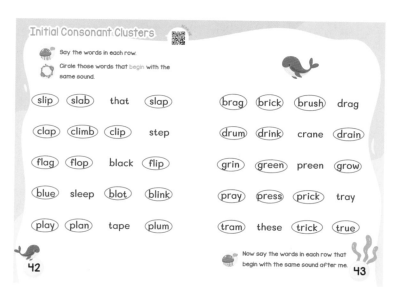

## Initial Consonant Clusters

Say the words in each row.

Circle those words that begin with the same sound.

| | | | |
|---|---|---|---|
| (slip) | (slab) | that | (slap) |
| (clap) | (climb) | (clip) | step |
| (flag) | (flop) | black | (flip) |
| (blue) | sleep | (blot) | (blink) |
| (play) | (plan) | tape | (plum) |

| | | | |
|---|---|---|---|
| (brag) | (brick) | (brush) | drag |
| (drum) | (drink) | crane | (drain) |
| (grin) | (green) | preen | (grow) |
| (pray) | (press) | (prick) | tray |
| (tram) | these | (trick) | (true) |

Now say the words in each row that begin with the same sound after me.

42

43

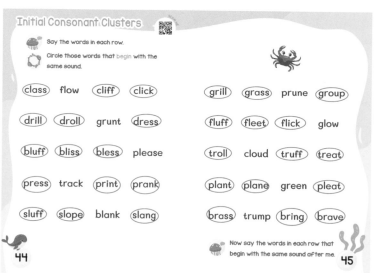

## Initial Consonant Clusters

Say the words in each row.

Circle those words that begin with the same sound.

| | | | |
|---|---|---|---|
| (class) | flow | (cliff) | (click) |
| (drill) | (droll) | grunt | (dress) |
| (bluff) | (bliss) | (bless) | please |
| (press) | track | (print) | (prank) |
| (sluff) | (slope) | blank | (slang) |

| | | | |
|---|---|---|---|
| (grill) | (grass) | prune | (group) |
| (fluff) | (fleet) | (flick) | glow |
| (troll) | cloud | (truff) | (treat) |
| (plant) | (plane) | green | (pleat) |
| (brass) | trump | (bring) | (brave) |

Now say the words in each row that begin with the same sound after me.

44

45

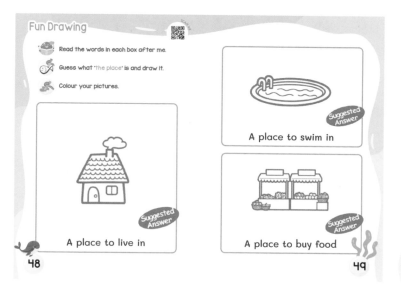

## Fun Drawing

Read the words in each box after me.

Guess what "the place" is and draw it.

Colour your pictures.

A place to live in

A place to swim in

*Suggested Answer*

A place to buy food

*Suggested Answer*

48

49

149

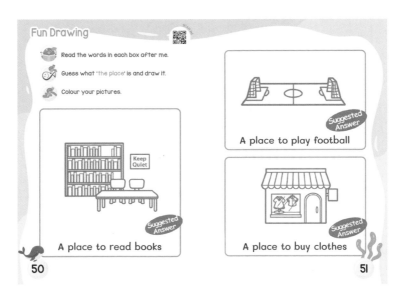

## Fun Drawing

- Read the words in each box after me.
- Guess what 'the place' is and draw it.
- Colour your pictures.

A place to read books

A place to play football

A place to buy clothes

50

51

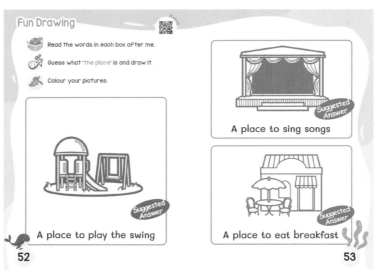

## Fun Drawing

- Read the words in each box after me.
- Guess what 'the place' is and draw it.
- Colour your pictures.

A place to play the swing

A place to sing songs

A place to eat breakfast

52

53

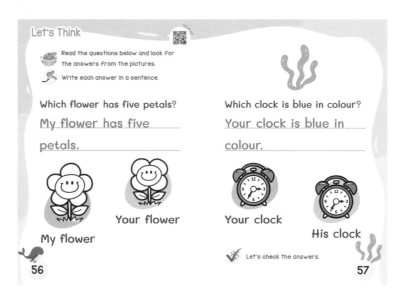

## Let's Think

- Read the questions below and look for the answers from the pictures.
- Write each answer in a sentence.

Which flower has five petals?

My flower has five petals.

Which clock is blue in colour?

Your clock is blue in colour.

My flower

Your flower

Your clock

His clock

Let's check the answers.

56

57

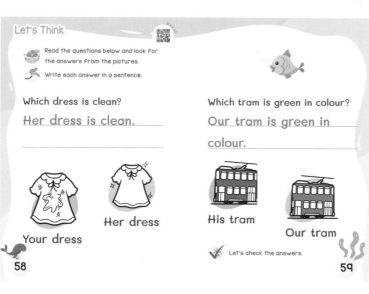

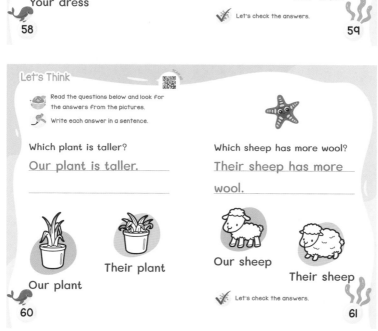

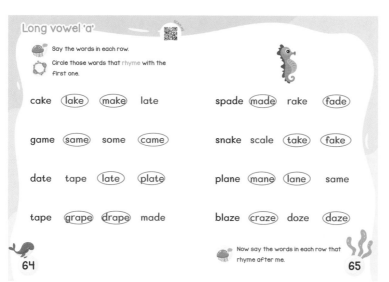

## Let's Think

Read the questions below and look for the answers from the pictures.

Write each answer in a sentence.

**Which dress is clean?**

Her dress is clean.

**Which tram is green in colour?**

Our tram is green in colour.

His tram

Our tram

Her dress

Your dress

Let's check the answers.

58

59

## Let's Think

Read the questions below and look for the answers from the pictures.

Write each answer in a sentence.

**Which plant is taller?**

Our plant is taller.

**Which sheep has more wool?**

Their sheep has more wool.

Their plant

Our plant

Our sheep

Their sheep

Let's check the answers.

60

61

## Long vowel 'a'

Say the words in each row.

Circle those words that rhyme with the first one.

cake (lake) (make) late        spade (made) rake (fade)

game (same) some (came)        snake scale (take) (fake)

date tape (late) (plate)        plane (mane) (lane) same

tape (grape) (drape) made        blaze (craze) doze (daze)

Now say the words in each row that rhyme after me.

64

65

151

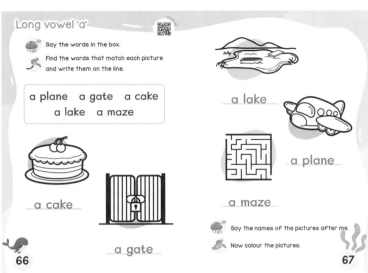

## Long vowel 'a'

- Say the words in the box.
- Find the words that match each picture and write them on the line.

a plane   a gate   a cake
a lake   a maze

a lake

a plane

a cake

a maze

a gate

- Say the names of the pictures after me.
- Now colour the pictures.

66

67

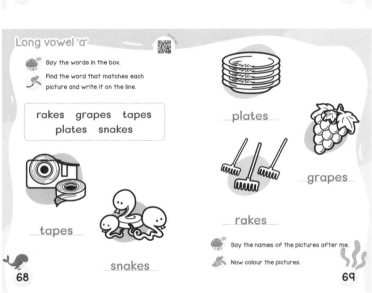

## Long vowel 'a'

- Say the words in the box.
- Find the word that matches each picture and write it on the line.

rakes   grapes   tapes
plates   snakes

plates

grapes

rakes

tapes

snakes

- Say the names of the pictures after me.
- Now colour the pictures.

68

69

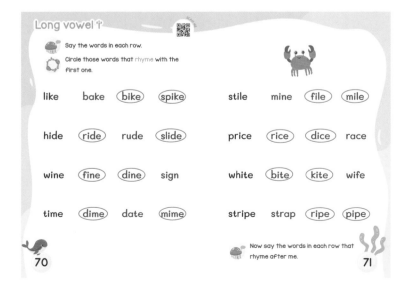

## Long vowel 'i'

- Say the words in each row.
- Circle those words that rhyme with the first one.

| like | bake | (bike) | (spike) | stile | mine | (file) | (mile) |
| hide | (ride) | rude | (slide) | price | (rice) | (dice) | race |
| wine | (fine) | (dine) | sign | white | (bite) | (kite) | wife |
| time | (dime) | date | (mime) | stripe | strap | (ripe) | (pipe) |

- Now say the words in each row that rhyme after me.

70

71

152

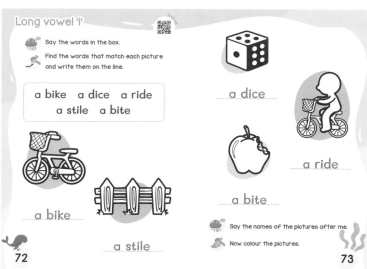

## Long vowel 'i'

Say the words in the box.

Find the words that match each picture and write them on the line.

a bike   a dice   a ride
a stile   a bite

a dice

a ride

a bite

Say the names of the pictures after me.

Now colour the pictures.

a bike

a stile

72

73

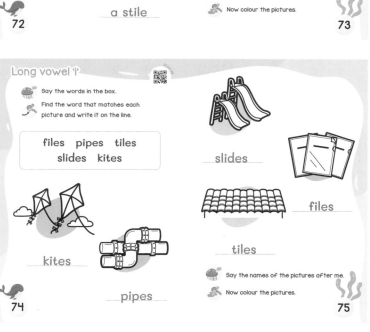

## Long vowel 'i'

Say the words in the box.

Find the word that matches each picture and write it on the line.

files   pipes   tiles
slides   kites

slides

files

tiles

Say the names of the pictures after me.

Now colour the pictures.

kites

pipes

74

75

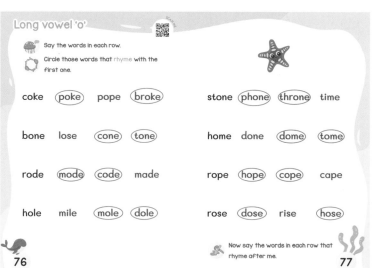

## Long vowel 'o'

Say the words in each row.

Circle those words that rhyme with the first one.

coke   (poke)   pope   (broke)

stone   (phone)   (throne)   time

bone   lose   (cone)   (tone)

home   done   (dome)   (tome)

rode   (mode)   (code)   made

rope   (hope)   (cope)   cape

hole   mile   (mole)   (dole)

rose   (dose)   rise   (hose)

Now say the words in each row that rhyme after me.

76

77

153

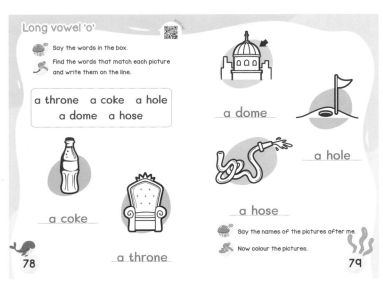

## Long vowel 'o'

Say the words in the box.

Find the words that match each picture and write them on the line.

a throne   a coke   a hole
a dome   a hose

a dome

a hole

a hose

a coke

a throne

Say the names of the pictures after me.

Now colour the pictures.

78

79

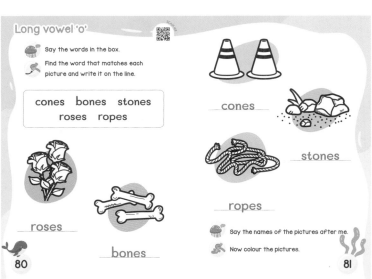

## Long vowel 'o'

Say the words in the box.

Find the word that matches each picture and write it on the line.

cones   bones   stones
roses   ropes

cones

stones

ropes

roses

bones

Say the names of the pictures after me.

Now colour the pictures.

80

81

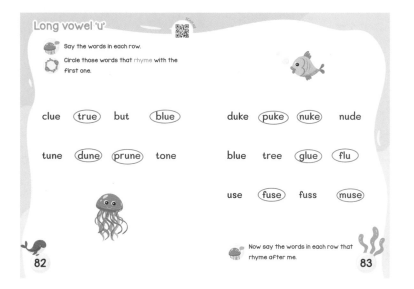

## Long vowel 'u'

Say the words in each row.

Circle those words that rhyme with the first one.

clue   (true)   but   (blue)          duke   (puke)   (nuke)   nude

tune   (dune)   (prune)   tone       blue   tree   (glue)   (flu)

use   (fuse)   fuss   (muse)

Now say the words in each row that rhyme after me.

82

83

154

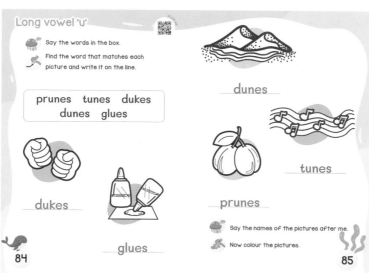

## Long vowel 'u'

🪼 Say the words in the box.

🫧 Find the word that matches each picture and write it on the line.

dunes

prunes   tunes   dukes
dunes   glues

tunes

dukes

prunes

🪼 Say the names of the pictures after me.

🫧 Now colour the pictures.

glues

84

85

## Fun Drawing

🪼 Read the words in each box after me.

🐟 Draw as you are told to do.

🫧 Colour your pictures.

Suggested Answer

There are two dogs.
Give each dog a bone.

Suggested Answer

There are five roses.
Colour them in five colours.

88

89

## Fun Drawing

🪼 Read the words in each box after me.

🐟 Draw as you are told to do.

🫧 Colour your pictures.

Suggested Answer

Jane wants to fly a kite.
Give her a kite.

Suggested Answer

Sue

Sue has baked a cake.
Write her name on it.

90

91

155

## Fun Drawing

🥣 Read the words in each box after me.

🎏 Draw as you are told to do.

🖌 Colour your pictures.

**Suggested Answer**

Watch out! There is a snake
in the hole.
Draw a snake in it.

92

**Suggested Answer**

Dave loves to drink coke.
Give him a coke.

93

## Fun Drawing

🥣 Read the words in each box after me.

🎏 Draw as you are told to do.

🖌 Colour your pictures.

**Suggested Answer**

There are two stones
on the table.
Draw four more stones on it.

94

**Suggested Answer**

There is a throne.
Draw a king sitting on it.

95

## Fun Drawing

🥣 Read the words in each box after me.

🎏 Draw as you are told to do.

🖌 Colour your pictures.

**Suggested Answer**

It is a fine day.
Draw a plane in the sky.

96

**Suggested Answer**

June likes to play on the slide.
Draw June on the slide.

97

156

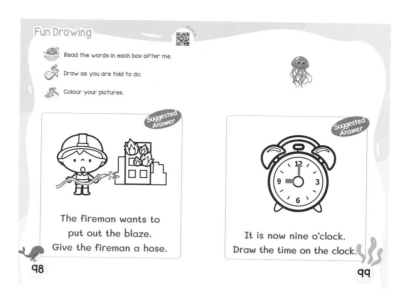

## Fun Drawing

Read the words in each box after me.

Draw as you are told to do.

Colour your pictures.

**Suggested Answer**

The fireman wants to put out the blaze. Give the fireman a hose.

98

**Suggested Answer**

It is now nine o'clock. Draw the time on the clock.

99

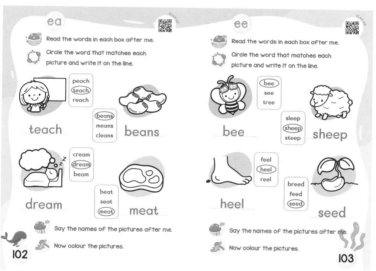

### ea

Read the words in each box after me.

Circle the word that matches each picture and write it on the line.

peach
(teach)
reach

teach

(beans)
means
cleans

beans

cream
(dream)
beam

dream

beat
seat
(meat)

meat

Say the names of the pictures after me.

Now colour the pictures.

102

### ee

Read the words in each box after me.

Circle the word that matches each picture and write it on the line.

bee
see
tree

bee

sleep
(sheep)
steep

sheep

feel
(heel)
reel

heel

breed
feed
(seed)

seed

Say the names of the pictures after me.

Now colour the pictures.

103

### ea   ee

Fill in the missing sounds of the words to make them all rhyme with each other.

The first one is done for you.

| sea | pea   tea | bean | mean   lean |
|     | flea |      | clean |

| meat | heat   beat | heel | feel   reel |
|      | seat |      | steel |

| see | bee   tree | beam | dream   cream |
|     | three |     | steam |

| feet | beet   meet | peep | sheep   sleep |
|      | fleet |     | steep |

Now say the rhyming words in each row after me.

104
105

157

## ai

🥣 Read the words in each box after me.

⚙️ Circle the word that matches each picture and write it on the line.

rain
(train)
vain

train

pail
tail
(snail)

snail

paint
faint
(saint)

saint

(chain)
drain
strain

chain

🐚 Say the names of the pictures after me.

🪥 Now colour the pictures.

106

## ay

🥣 Read the words in each box after me.

⚙️ Circle the word that matches each picture and write it on the line.

say
(tray)
day

tray

bay
way
(clay)

clay

may
stay
(play)

play

(spray)
pray
stray

spray

🐚 Say the names of the pictures after me.

🪥 Now colour the pictures.

107

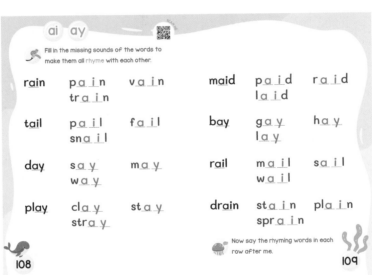

## ai ay

🖊️ Fill in the missing sounds of the words to make them all rhyme with each other.

rain    p a i n    v a i n
         tr a i n

maid    p a i d    r a i d
         l a i d

tail    p a i l    f a i l
         sn a i l

bay    g a y    h a y
         l a y

day    s a y    m a y
         w a y

rail    m a i l    s a i l
         w a i l

play    cl a y    st a y
         str a y

drain    st a i n    pl a i n
         spr a i n

🐚 Now say the rhyming words in each row after me.

108

109

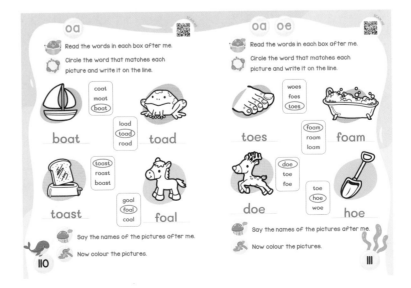

## oa

🥣 Read the words in each box after me.

⚙️ Circle the word that matches each picture and write it on the line.

coat
moat
(boat)

boat

load
(toad)
road

toad

(toast)
roast
boast

toast

goal
(foal)
coal

foal

🐚 Say the names of the pictures after me.

🪥 Now colour the pictures.

110

## oa oe

🥣 Read the words in each box after me.

⚙️ Circle the word that matches each picture and write it on the line.

woes
foes
(toes)

toes

(foam)
roam
loam

foam

(doe)
toe
foe

doe

toe
(hoe)
woe

hoe

🐚 Say the names of the pictures after me.

🪥 Now colour the pictures.

111

Fill in the missing sounds of the words to make them all rhyme with each other.

**coat**    b o a t    m o a t    g o a t

**road**    t o a d    l o a d    g o a d

**toe**    f o e    w o e    d o e

**woes**    d o e s    t o e s    f o e s

**loam**    f o a m    r o a m

**foal**    go a l    c o a l

**moan**    l o a n    gr o a n

**roast**    bo a st    c o a st

Now say the rhyming words in each row after me.

112

113

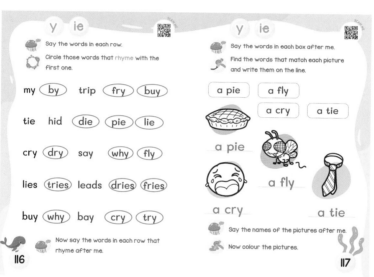

Say the words in each row.

Circle those words that rhyme with the first one.

my  (by)  trip  (fry)  (buy)

tie  hid  (die)  (pie)  (lie)

cry  (dry)  say  (why)  (fly)

lies  (tries)  leads  (dries)  (fries)

buy  (why)  bay  (cry)  (try)

Now say the words in each row that rhyme after me.

116

Say the words in each box after me.

Find the words that match each picture and write them on the line.

a pie    a fly

a cry    a tie

a pie

a fly

a cry    a tie

Say the names of the pictures after me.

Now colour the pictures.

117

Say the sentence in each box.

Find the sentence that matches each picture and write it on the line.

He tries on the tie.

She buys a pie.

She buys a pie.

118

He tries on the tie.

Say the sentences after me.

Now colour the pictures.

119

159

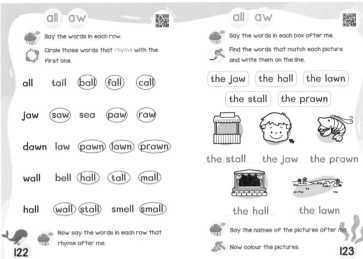

## all aw

Say the words in each row.

Circle those words that rhyme with the first one.

all    tail    (ball) (fall) (call)

jaw    (saw)    sea    (paw) (raw)

dawn    law    (pawn) (lawn) (prawn)

wall    bell    (hall) (tall) (mall)

hall    (wall) (stall)    smell    (small)

Now say the words in each row that rhyme after me.

122

## all aw

Say the words in each box after me.

Find the words that match each picture and write them on the line.

the jaw    the hall    the lawn

the stall    the prawn

the stall    the jaw    the prawn

the hall    the lawn

Say the names of the pictures after me.

Now colour the pictures.

123

## Rhyming Words

Say the words in each box after me.

Find the words that match each picture and write them on the line.

A tall wall falls

A small prawn on the lawn

a small prawn on the lawn

a tall wall falls

Say the words after me.

Now colour the pictures.

124

125

## Quiz 14.1

The words in each row rhyme with each other.

Write another word that rhymes with them on the line.

bee    see    tree / three

foe    woe    toe / hoe

say    may    way / bay

pea    tea    flea / sea

rail    pail    mail / sail

load    road    toad / goad

boat    moat    float / goat

peep    sheep    creep / steep

Suggested Answer

Suggested Answer

Check your answers with the answer key.

Score /8

128

129

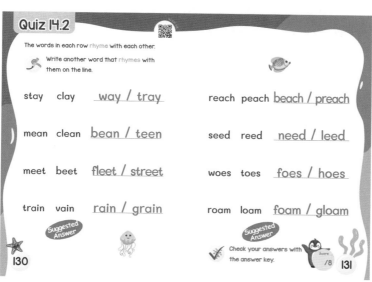

## Quiz 14.2

The words in each row rhyme with each other.

Write another word that rhymes with them on the line.

| | | |
|---|---|---|
| stay | clay | __way / tray__ |
| mean | clean | __bean / teen__ |
| meet | beet | __fleet / street__ |
| train | vain | __rain / grain__ |

*Suggested Answer*

130

| | | |
|---|---|---|
| reach | peach | __beach / preach__ |
| seed | reed | __need / leed__ |
| woes | toes | __foes / hoes__ |
| roam | loam | __foam / gloam__ |

*Suggested Answer*

Check your answers with the answer key.

Score /8    131

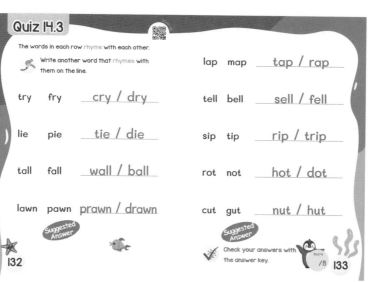

## Quiz 14.3

The words in each row rhyme with each other.

Write another word that rhymes with them on the line.

| | | |
|---|---|---|
| try | fry | __cry / dry__ |
| lie | pie | __tie / die__ |
| tall | fall | __wall / ball__ |
| lawn | pawn | __prawn / drawn__ |

*Suggested Answer*

132

| | | |
|---|---|---|
| lap | map | __tap / rap__ |
| tell | bell | __sell / fell__ |
| sip | tip | __rip / trip__ |
| rot | not | __hot / dot__ |
| cut | gut | __nut / hut__ |

*Suggested Answer*

Check your answers with the answer key.

Score /8    133

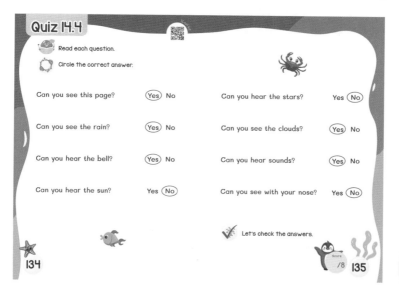

## Quiz 14.4

Read each question.

Circle the correct answer.

| | | |
|---|---|---|
| Can you see this page? | (Yes) No | |
| Can you see the rain? | (Yes) No | |
| Can you hear the bell? | (Yes) No | |
| Can you hear the sun? | Yes (No) | |

| | | |
|---|---|---|
| Can you hear the stars? | Yes (No) | |
| Can you see the clouds? | (Yes) No | |
| Can you hear sounds? | (Yes) No | |
| Can you see with your nose? | Yes (No) | |

Let's check the answers.

134

Score /8    135

161

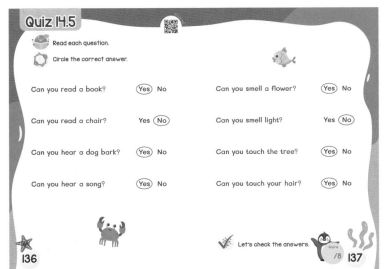

## Quiz 14.5

Read each question.

Circle the correct answer.

| | | | |
|---|---|---|---|
| Can you read a book? | (Yes) No | Can you smell a flower? | (Yes) No |
| Can you read a chair? | Yes (No) | Can you smell light? | Yes (No) |
| Can you hear a dog bark? | (Yes) No | Can you touch the tree? | (Yes) No |
| Can you hear a song? | (Yes) No | Can you touch your hair? | (Yes) No |

Let's check the answers. Score /8

136    137

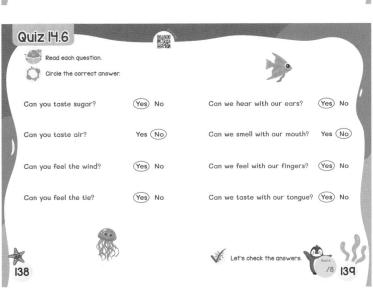

## Quiz 14.6

Read each question.

Circle the correct answer.

| | | | |
|---|---|---|---|
| Can you taste sugar? | (Yes) No | Can we hear with our ears? | (Yes) No |
| Can you taste air? | Yes (No) | Can we smell with our mouth? | Yes (No) |
| Can you feel the wind? | (Yes) No | Can we feel with our fingers? | (Yes) No |
| Can you feel the tie? | (Yes) No | Can we taste with our tongue? | (Yes) No |

Let's check the answers. Score /8

138    139

162